© 1985 Little Star Publishing Ltd., Great Britain
all rights reserved
This 1988 edition published by Derrydale Books
Distributed by Crown Publishers, Inc.
225 Park Avenue South, New York, New York 10003
Printed and Bound in Italy

ISBN 0-517-66779-7

hgfedcba

WHO WANTS TO ADOPT
PADDY
THE PLAYFUL
PUPPY

Derrydale Books

New York

The large farm house stood in the middle of well tended farm land. Close to the farmyard was the farmer's house. The farmer himself was a great sportsman, and Paddy was his gun dog's puppy.

In the absence of his father, the puppy grew under his mother's watchful eye.

However, he was often glum, for his mother forbade him many things: "Don't bark loudly! Stay here! Don't run like that! You'll hurt yourself!"

And so, though he was a strong pup and full of energy, he was expected to keep calm and not get excited.

And that fateful day, after their meal, his mother lay down for a snooze, saying:

"Don't disturb me! Don't cause an uproar!"

But Paddy could stand it no longer and, careful not to awaken his mother, he tiptoed away from the kennel.

"Surely, somewhere else, I'll find someone to play with!"

Beyond the yard that had been the limits of his world, lay the farmyard.

Paddy saw that the wooden gate had been left half-open, and he happily ran through to the other side of the fence. He soon met someone. Mommy Goose's baby geese.

"Bow, wow!" he barked, meaning "Will you play with me?"

"Qua! Qua! Qua!" shouted the baby geese, saying "We'll play! We'll play!"

So the puppy began to play gaily with his new friends, till in his excitement, he knocked one of the baby geese over with his paw.

"Quaaaa! Quaa!" squawked the baby geese meaning "Help! Help!"

When Mommy Goose heard her baby's cry for help, she rushed furiously up with stretched neck and harsh beak ready to chase the intruder.

Poor Paddy! He'll have to find new playmates!

Still stinging from Mommy Goose's pecking, Paddy ran and ran, farther and farther away from the farm, till he came to a flock of sheep.

"Baa! Baa!" bleated the sheep, welcoming him to the flock.

The little dog strolled among the sheep, carefully sniffing their strong smell.

A curious lamb went over to him. Like Paddy, he was looking for a playmate. Paddy circled the lamb, sniffing him from head to foot, while the little creature patiently waited for the puppy to finish his inspection.

"Will you play with me?" Paddy asked.

"Yes," said the lamb, happily.

Suddenly a fearful snarl interrupted the conversation. Paddy felt a pair of strong jaws seize him by the scruff of the nech and carry him away, dangling in the air, from the flock.

"Don't go near the sheep again! Is that clear?" growled the fierce-eyed German sheepdog who was guarding the flock.

"I'm so sorry," murmured the puppy feebly.

A little way off, Paddy suddenly heard a braying sound. When he crept quietly along to see who was making the sound he found a small donkey tied to a tree.

The two animals stared at each other in amazement. Paddy had never set eyes on a donkey before and the only dog the donkey had ever seen was the sheepdog.

The puppy walked around the donkey, wondering if this was a likely playmate. But a big bumble bee ruined everything.

It buzzed around and around the donkey's nose, frightening the animal, which started to buck and kick.

And without ever knowing the reason why, Paddy was propelled by a mighty kick several yards away. He hurried away feeling very upset.

"Hee haw! Hee haw!" brayed the donkey, who wanted to play, but the puppy only shook his head and yelped:

"You're not terribly friendly!"

A cow was grazing quietly in a nearby meadow. "Ding dong, ding dong" went the cowbell every time the contented cow lowered her head to crop the grass. She raised her large gentle eyes to look at the puppy, sitting watching her.

"What do you want?" she mumbled between mouthfuls.

"I want to play," said Paddy, hopefully.

"Play? Hmm! I'm grazing now. I haven't time now to play, said the cow.

"If you want, I can wait" the puppy insisted.

"Hmmm! I don't think I'm the right playmate for you. I might have enjoyed it when I was younger. But now, mmmm, I have to concentrate on eating so I can produce plenty of milk!"

And she slowly moved away to where the grass grew more thickly. Farther on, a nanny goat hat been tied to a large tree.

When she moved, Paddy noticed the movement, and when he saw she was tied, he recalled his adventure with the donkey.

"This time, I'll keep away from her hind legs, so that I don't get kicked!" the clever puppy said to himself.

The nanny goat, however, was in a bad mood. She had been tied to the tree for hours and, with lowered head, scowled suspiciously at the newcomer.

Paddy was on the point of suggesting, as usual, that they might play together, when a glint in the staring red eyes made him think twice.

"Would she want to play?" Paddy asked himself, hesitating.

The nanny goat simply took one step forward, head well down, and charged.

Poor Paddy took to his heels and ran out of the way.

Sadly, the puppy turned back in the direction of the farm. He came to a low wall. Propping his paws against it, he tried to peer over, but the wall was too high. However, a nearby bale of straw helped him to scramble over.

How lovely! There was a pen full of rabbits of all sizes and colors, nibbling away, hopping about, and playing with each other. "At last, someone to play with! Now, I'll ask if I may join in their fun!" So he opened his mouth and barked:

"Bow, wow!"

There was a sudden rush, as all the startled rabbits scattered in search of a hiding place.

"Bow, wow!" Paddy went on, but nobody answered his call.

It took him quite a few tries before he managed to scramble back over the wall. Just as he was about to jump to the ground, he saw another dog in the distance. He dashed towards it, saying to himself:

"What a beatiful dog! He's even more handsome than Father or the sheepdog, almost more beautiful than Mother, too!"

This time, the puppy received a less harsh welcome. The tall dog elegantly sniffed the small pup, before loftily asking:

"Where are you from?"

"From the farm over there."

"What's your father?"

"He's a gun dog. A very good one, really smart!"

"Hmm! Is everyone in your family as small as you are?"

Now, this remark rather surprised Paddy. He'd never thought about size before.

"Well, actually... I'm still a puppy..." He thought of his father and mother who were not tall dogs.

"Why are you so tall?" he asked the other.

"I'm a collie. I'm an aristocratic dog and my owners keep me as a companion for their little girl."

"Do you play with her?"

"Sometimes, but I really prefer it when she brushes my coat. Do you see what a lovely thick silky coat I have?"

Paddy looked sorrowfully down at his own short rough coat and tried to change the subject.

"Would you play with me?" he asked timidly.

The tall dog tossed his head, without saying a word, so Paddy got up the courage to ask:

"You don't know where I can find a playmate, do you?"

The collie glanced doubtfully at the cocker spaniel puppy, thought briefly, then said:

"Go straight on, to the yellow field down there. There ought to be a foal in the paddock, unless he's been taken away. Try him! He should be about your own age!"

As Paddy went off, the collie added:

"Remind the foal to say hello to his father for me. We were great friends when my little mistress used to..."

But Paddy was already out of earshot.

The foal whinnied with delight when he saw Paddy and cantered around the happily barking puppy.

He pushed Paddy head over heels with his damp muzzle, then said:

"Race me!"

Paddy dashed joyfully after the galloping foal.

"Stop for a minute!" he barked, his heart beating wildly after such a fast run.

But the restless foal galloped up and down, urging the puppy to race, till Paddy flopped into the grass, quite exhausted, with his tongue hanging out.

"I can't go on!" he gasped, "I'm tired!"

Dusk had begun to fall, and a hollow feeling in his tummy reminded Paddy of dinner back at the kennel.

He set off toward home.

Suddenly, he sniffed the air, he could smell the familiar scent of a dog's dinner.

Following the invisible trail, he quickly reached the farmyard, where the German sheepdog's family was already around a large dish. Paddy trotted closer, hoping to be offered a bite, but a warning growl kept him at a distance. From afar, Paddy watched while the sheepdog puppies gobbled their dinner. His mouth was watering, but the watchful stare in the sheepdog's eyes kept Paddy away. Since the dogs had eyes for only their meal, a kitten thought it would be safe to explore the kennel. Paddy ran after her to say hello.

"Don't run away! Come back!" cried the puppy to the frightened kitten. But the kitten ran as fast as she could, away from the puppy close at her heels. Suddenly she stopped, instinctively whipping out her claws to face what looked like real danger.

"Don't run away! I won't hurt you!" said Paddy again, keeping out of range of the kitten's claws.

The kitten lost her fear when she realized that Paddy meant no harm, and they began to chat.

At a certain point, it was the kitten who asked Paddy:

"Why don't you dogs like cats?„

Paddy stood in silence for a moment, then replied:

"Maybe it is their smell."

"Why, do you think I smell?" demanded the kitten.

"Well, no. Not really!"

"Why, then?"

"My father says that you cats like living close to people, and because you're selfish, you don't want people to have dogs around, too."

The kitten quickly retorted.

"Now! You've taken the very words out of my mouth! My mother told me exactly the same thing about dogs!"

Paddy thought for a bit, then wisely replied:

"Well, if our parents think the very same things about each other, then they must be wrong, mustn't they?"

The kitten quickly replied.

"Of course they're wrong! But *we're* friends, aren't we?"

Overhead, the leaves rustled, and a pair of green eyes coldly stared at Paddy.

"It's my mother," whispered the kitten, "I must rush!"

"I'd better rush, too!" exclaimed Paddy.

He watched the kitten scramble clumsily up the tree under her mother's keen eye.

"I'm always telling you not to speak to dogs..." he could hear the voice in the leaves. But the kitten's little face peeped through again to say goodbye.

"Bye, bye! See you soon..."

Paddy was practically home and by this time a comforting scent was his guide. It was that of his mother still tied to the kennel's iron ring, waiting for him.

Paddy hung his head, begging forgiveness for being away for so long. But there was no trace of anger in his mother's kindly eyes.

"Come and have your dinner," she said, "It's late!" And with a gentle pat of a large paw, she nudged the puppy into the kennel.

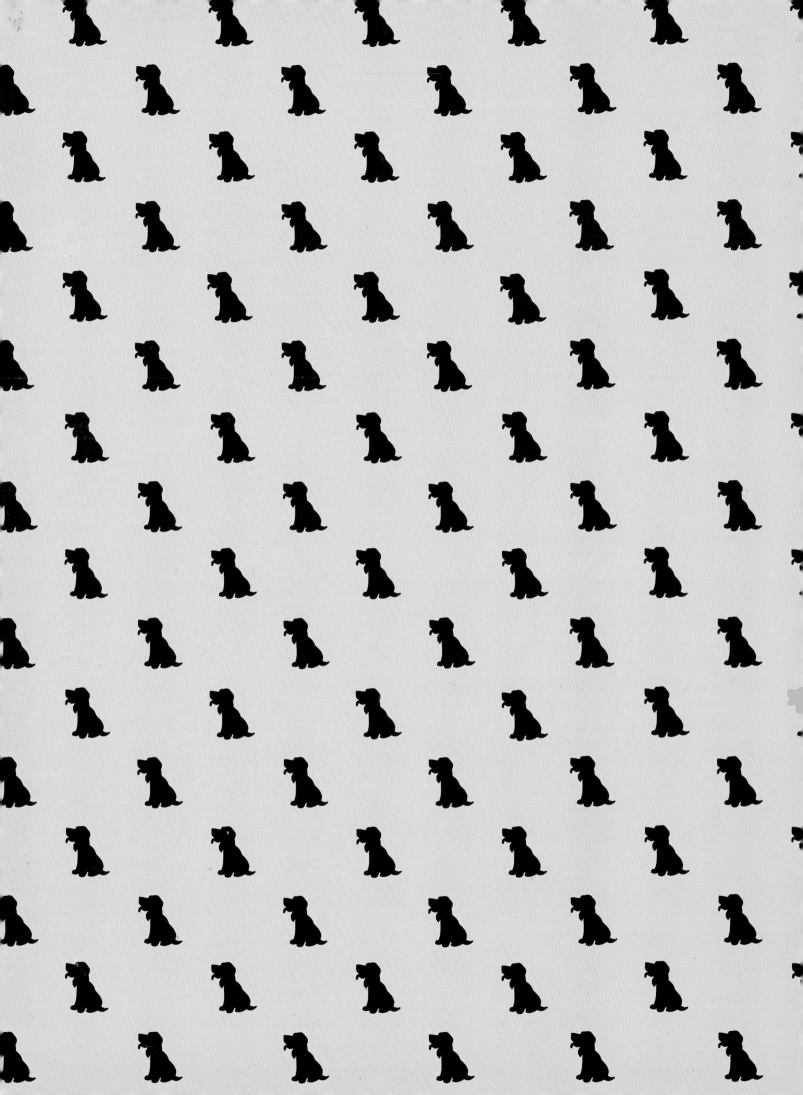